*The children loved their new life in the little house
beside the railway. They made friends with the
Station Master and the Porter, and gave special
names to all the trains. Only one thing spoiled it. Why
didn't Father come back to them?*

Published by Ladybird Books Ltd Loughborough Leicestershire UK
Ladybird Books Inc Lewiston Maine 04240 USA

THE RAILWAY CHILDREN

by Edith Nesbit

retold by Joan Collins

illustrated by Kathie Layfield

Ladybird Books

The Beginning of Things

They were not railway children to begin with. They lived near London, with their father and mother, in a red brick villa with coloured glass in the front door, lots of white paint, and what house advertisements call 'every modern convenience'. The only times they travelled by train were to go to the Zoo or Madame Tussaud's.

There were three of them. Roberta, the eldest, was perhaps her mother's secret favourite. Peter wanted to be an engineer. Phyllis meant well, but sometimes things seemed to go wrong for her.

They had a dog called James, and a mother who read stories to them, helped them with their homework and wrote funny poems for their birthdays. Their father was just perfect – never cross, never unfair, and always ready for fun.

They were perfectly happy until, one day, a dreadful change came into their lives.

Late one evening, two men called to see their father, who was busy mending a toy railway engine for Peter. Then a taxi was ordered and Father went away in it. Their mother looked as white as a sheet, and very

upset. She asked the children just to be good,
and not to ask questions.

The children did their best to help, though
they did not quite know how. Roberta realised
that something serious was making her
mother miserable.

'I say,' said Phyllis, 'you used to say it was
so dull – nothing happening like in books. Now
something *has* happened!'

'I never wanted things to happen to make
Mother unhappy,' said Roberta. 'Everything's
perfectly horrid.'

Everything continued to be perfectly horrid for some weeks. Then they were told that their father had gone away on business – he worked for the Government – and might be away a long time. Mother said, 'Don't worry! It'll all come right in the end!'

She told them they were going away to live in a little white house in the country. All the household things were packed, even the blankets and saucepans.

'We're taking all the ugly things, Mother,' said Roberta.

'We're taking the useful ones,' said her mother. 'We've got to play at being poor for a bit, my chickabiddy.'

When all the ugly useful things had been packed up in a van, a cab came to take the children to the station. It was such a long journey, they went to sleep on the train, till Mother shook them gently and said, 'Wake up, dears, we're here.'

They stood on the draughty platform and watched the tail lights of the guard's van disappear into the darkness. They did not guess then how they would grow to love the railway, and how soon it would become the centre of their new life.

It was a long, dark, muddy walk from the station to their new home, and Phyllis's bootlaces kept coming undone. She had to keep stopping to tie them.

The rough country road went through a gate in the fields to a dark lumpish thing Mother said was the house, Three Chimneys.

There were no lights, and the front door was locked. The carter, who brought their luggage, found the key under the doorstep, and lighted a candle for them on the kitchen table. The kitchen was dark and forbidding, with furniture piled up in the corners, and no fire in the grate.

They could hear a rustling and scampering in the walls. 'What's that noise?' asked the girls. 'Only the rats,' said the carter, going out. As the door shut after him, the draught blew out the candle.

'I wish we'd never come!' wailed Phyllis.
'Only the rats!' said Peter in the dark.

Peter's Coal Mine

'What fun!' said Mother. 'You've often wanted something to happen, and now it has. This is quite an adventure!'

A neighbour was supposed to have left them some supper, but they could not find any food. So they looked for their packing cases, which were in the cellar, and Mother managed to break one open with the kitchen poker. There were some odds and ends of food in it from the store-cupboard at home, so they had a picnic meal in the kitchen.

Everyone was very tired, but cheered up at the sight of the funny, but delightful supper. There were plain and fancy biscuits, sardines, preserved ginger, cooking raisins, candied peel and marmalade, all washed down with ginger wine and water, out of tea-cups.

They all helped to make the beds, and went to sleep. Roberta woke up in the night and could hear her mother still moving about in her bedroom.

Next morning, the children woke early, and crept down, mousy quiet, to get everything ready for breakfast before Mother woke up.

There was no water in the bedroom, so they washed, as much as they thought necessary, under the spout of the pump in the yard.

'It's much more fun than basin washing!' said Roberta. 'How sparkly the weeds are between the stones!'

They lit the fire, put the kettle on, and laid the table. Then they went out to explore.

The house stood in a field, on a hilly slope.
Down below, they could see the line of the
railway, and the black yawning mouth of a
tunnel. The station was out of sight. There
was a great bridge with tall arches running
across one end of the valley.

They all sat down on a great flat stone in
the grass, to watch for trains. Mother found
them, at eight o'clock, deeply asleep in a
contented, sun-warmed bunch.

By that time, the fire had burned out and
the kettle had boiled dry. But Mother had
found their supper laid in another room, so
they had it for breakfast — cold roast beef,
bread and butter, cheese and apple pie.

All the unpacking was done by late
afternoon, and Mother went to lie down. So
the children set off for the railway.

They slid down the short smooth turf slope, set with furze bushes and yellow rocks here and there. The way ended in a steep run and a wooden fence, and there was the railway, with shining metal rails, telegraph wires, posts and signals.

Suddenly, there was a rumbling sound, and a train rushed out of the tunnel with a shriek and snort, and slid noisily past them. They felt the rush of its passing. The stones between the lines jumped and rattled.

'Oh!' said Roberta. 'It was like a great dragon passing by!'

'I never thought we should ever get so near to a train as this!' gasped Peter.

'I wonder if that train's going to London? That's where Father is!' said Bobbie. (Everyone called her that.)

'Let's go to the station and find out,' said Peter.

They walked along the edge of the line, pretending the sleepers were stepping stones. The telegraph wires hummed overhead. They arrived at the station, by the sloping platform end, instead of the booking office, and peeped into the porter's room. He was half asleep, reading a newspaper.

13

There were a great many crossing lines at the station. Some were just sidings with trucks standing in them. In one of these there was a great heap, built like a solid wall, of square pieces of coal, with a line of whitewash at the top. The gong over the station door tingled twice, and the porter came out. He told them that the white mark was to show how much coal was there, so that they would know if anyone 'nicked' it.

'So don't you go off with none in your pockets, young gentleman!' (Peter was to remember this warning later.)

The children quickly settled down to their

new life in the country. There was so much to interest them. There was the canal with old horses plodding along the tow path dragging barges. The arched bridge that carried the water across the valley was called an aqueduct and was just like the pictures in Roberta's *History of Rome*. Above all, there was the railway.

Their old life seemed like a dream. They got used to being without Father, though they did not forget him. Their mother spent most of the day writing stories, and she sent them away to editors. Sometimes they came back, but sometimes a sensible editor kept one, and then they had halfpenny buns for tea.

Mother often reminded them that they were quite poor now. On a cold day in June, they asked for a fire, and she said, 'Coal is so dear! Go and have a good romp in the attic, that will warm you up!'

This gave Peter an idea, but he would not tell the others. 'It may be wrong, so I won't drag you into it,' he said. 'It's my lone adventure, but if Mother asks what I'm doing, say I'm playing at mines.'

'What sort of mines?'

'*Coal* mines! But don't tell on pain of torture!'

Two nights later, he called the girls to help him, and bring the Roman Chariot. (This was an old pram they had found in a shed.) They guided it down the slope towards the station. In a hollow, covered with bracken and heather, Peter showed them a small heap of coal.

'This is from St Peter's Mine!' he said, and they hauled it home in the chariot.

Mrs Viney, their daily help, remarked how well the coal was holding out that week!

But one dreadful night, Peter was caught by the Station Master, who lay in wait, like a cat by a mousehole. He found Peter scrabbling around in the coal heap with the white line around it.

'I'm not a thief!' said Peter indignantly. 'I'm a coal miner!' Bobbie and Phyllis, who had been hiding behind a truck, came bravely out to join Peter.

'Why, it's a whole gang of you!' exclaimed the Station Master. 'The children from Three Chimneys! Don't you know it's wrong to steal? What made you do such a thing?'

Peter explained how his mother had said they were too poor to have a fire. He thought it wasn't wrong to take coal from the *middle* of the pile – it was like mining.

The kindly Station Master promised to overlook it 'this once'. 'But you remember, stealing *is* stealing, even if you call it mining! Run along home!'

'You're a brick!' said Peter.

'You're a dear!' said Bobbie.

'You're a darling!' said Phyllis.

'That's all right!' said the Station Master.

The Old Gentleman

The children could not keep away from the railway. In the sleepy countryside the only things that went by were the trains, to which they gave names. The 9.15 up was The Green Dragon. The midnight express was The Fearsome Fly by Night.

Soon they made a friend, a fresh-faced old gentleman who travelled on the 9.15. He waved to them with his newspaper, when they stood on the railings to watch the Green Dragon tear out of its dark lair in the tunnel.

They waved rather grubby handkerchiefs back. They liked to think that perhaps he knew their father in London and would take their love to him.

On a halfpenny bun day, they mentioned to the Station Master that their mother had sold a story. He said they ought to be proud of having such a clever mother, and invited them to visit the station whenever they liked. So they knew he had forgiven them about the coal.

The Porter, whose name was Perks, told them all sorts of fascinating things about trains. You were only allowed to pull the communication cord if you were going to be murdered or something. An old lady had pulled it once because she thought it was the refreshment car bell and ordered a Bath bun when the guard came. Also Perks told them about the different kinds of engines. Peter started to collect engine numbers in a notebook.

One day their mother was taken ill, and Peter had to fetch the doctor from the village. He said it was influenza, and gave her some medicine. He also said she should have beef tea, brandy and all sorts of luxuries. The children were very worried.

'We've got to do something!' said Bobbie. 'Let's think *hard*!' At last they had an idea. They got a sheet and made a big notice, printed with blacking (the kind you use on the grate). It read: LOOK OUT AT THE STATION.

They fixed it up on the fence, and when the train went by, Peter pointed at it. Phyllis ran ahead to the station with a letter for the old gentleman. (She nearly missed him because her bootlace came undone again!)

The letter told how ill their mother was, and what they needed, and promised to repay him when they grew up. The old gentleman read it, smiled, and put it in his pocket. Then he went on reading *The Times*.

That evening Perks the Porter came to their door with a big hamper. In it was everything they had asked for, and much more – peaches, two chickens, port wine, red roses and a bottle of Eau-de-Cologne.

There was also a letter from the old gentleman. He said it was a pleasure to help, and their mother was not to be cross with them for asking.

A fortnight later, another notice went up. SHE IS NEARLY WELL THANK YOU.

Mother *was* very angry at first, but she knew the children had only wanted to help.

'You must never, never, *never* ask strangers to give us things!' she said earnestly. 'But I must write to thank your old gentleman for his kindness.'

Bobbie's Birthday

Family birthdays had always been special days at home. Though there was no money to buy presents now, Mother, Peter and Phyllis did not forget Bobbie's twelfth birthday.

It was a great surprise. She had to wait till a bell rang for her to come in to the dining room at tea-time.

The table was decorated with a lovely pattern of flowers to represent a map of the railway.

'Look! Those lilac lines are the metals!' said Peter. 'The station's done in brown wallflowers. The laburnum is the train, and those three red daisies are us, waving to the old gentleman. That's him, the pansy, in the laburnum train!'

Mother had made up a special song –

'Our darling Roberta,
No sorrow shall hurt her
If we can prevent it
Her whole life long.
Her birthday's our fête day,
We'll make it a great day,
And give her our presents,
And sing her our song.'

Phyllis had made her a needle case. Mother

gave her a silver brooch in the shape of a
buttercup. Peter shared his toy engine with
her, and put sweets in the tender.

There were twelve candles on the cake,
which had 'BOBBIE' on it in pink letters, and
she was given a forget-me-not crown to wear.
Then they played Blind Man's Bluff and
Mother read them a story.

'Don't stay up late, Mother, will you?' said
Bobbie anxiously.

'No, I'll just write to Father and go to bed.'

But much later, Bobbie crept down, to fetch
her presents, and found Mother, with her head
on her arms, at the table. It was rather good
of Bobbie to slip quietly away. 'She doesn't
want me to know she's unhappy,' she thought.
But it made a sad end to the birthday.

Prisoners and Captives

One day, Mother went to Maidbridge, the nearest town. She always went there to post her letters. The children went to meet her train, an hour before time, in the rain, and played games in the General Waiting Room.

The up train came in, and the children went to talk to their friend the engine driver, who had mended Peter's broken engine. They were surprised to see a crowd on the platform, around a man who looked ill and was talking in a foreign language.

It wasn't French or Latin or German. Nobody could understand it. The man had long hair and wild eyes and he was trembling. Peter asked him, 'Parlay voo Frongsay?'

The man poured out a flood of words Peter knew were French, though he did not understand them.

All the children had been *taught* French at school. How they wished they had *learned* it! But their mother could talk French and she would be here on the next train.

Bobbie begged the Station Master not to frighten the man. 'His eyes look like a fox's in a trap!'

'I think I ought to send for the police,' said the Station Master.

Peter had a bright idea and showed him some foreign stamps. He picked out a Russian stamp and nodded. Just then Mother's train came in.

She spoke French rapidly and the stranger replied excitedly. Then she said, 'It's all right. He's a Russian and he's lost his ticket. I'm going to take him home with me and I'll tell you more in the morning. He's a great man in his own country. He writes books – beautiful books – I've read some of them.'

The children rushed home to light a fire and fetch the doctor. Mother took some clothes out of a trunk. They were Father's. Bobbie felt terrible. She asked her mother if Father was dead.

Mother gave her a hug. 'Daddy is quite well. He'll come back to us some day. Don't worry, darling.'

That night Mother told them about the Russian gentleman. He had written a book about the poor people in Russia in the time of the Tsar, and how the rich people ought to help them. Because of this, he was put in prison and then sent to Siberia, where he was very badly treated.

'How did he get away?'

Prisoners were allowed to go as soldiers during the war, and he deserted. He heard his wife and child had come to England, so he came to look for them in London. On the way he lost his ticket and got out at the wrong station.

'Do you think he'll find his family?'

'I hope and pray so,' said Mother. Then, after a pause, she said, 'Dears, when you say your prayers, ask God to pity *all* prisoners and captives.'

'To pity' Bobbie repeated slowly, '*all* prisoners and captives. Is that right?'

'Yes,' said Mother, 'to pity *all* prisoners and captives.'

Saviours of the Train

The Russian gentleman was soon well
enough to sit out in the garden. Mother wrote
to Members of Parliament and other people
whom she thought might know where his
family was. The children could not talk with
him, but they showed their friendship by
smiling and bringing him flowers.

One day they had the idea of fetching him
wild cherries that grew along the cliff by the
mouth of the tunnel. When they got to the top
of the cutting, they looked down to where the
railway lines lay.

It was like a mountain gorge, with bushes and trees overhanging the cutting. A narrow 'ladder' of wooden steps led down to the line, with a swing gate at the top. They were almost at the gate when Bobbie cried, 'Hush! Stop! What's that?'

'That' was a sort of rustling, whispering sound. It stopped, and then started again, louder and more like a rumbling. 'Look at that tree over there!' cried Peter.

A tree with grey leaves and white flowers seemed to be moving, shivering and walking down the slope. Then all the trees seemed to be sliding towards the railway line.

'What is it? I don't like it!' cried Phyllis. 'Let's go home!'

'It's all coming down,' said Peter. As he spoke, the great rock on the top of which the trees grew leaned slowly forward. The walking trees stood still and shivered. Then rock, grass, trees and bushes slipped right away from the face of the cutting and fell on the line with a crash that could be heard half a mile away. A cloud of dust came up.

'It's right across the down line!' said Phyllis.

'The 11.29's due!' said Peter. 'We must let them know at the station, or there'll be a frightful accident!'

'There's not enough time,' said Bobbie. 'What can we do? We ought to wave a red flag!'

The girls were wearing red flannel petticoats! They hurriedly took them off and ripped them in pieces, so that they had six flags. Peter made flagpoles from saplings and made holes to stick them through. Then they stood ready, each with two flags, waiting for the train.

Bobbie thought that no one would notice the silly little flags, and everyone would be killed. Then came the distant rumble and hum of the metals, and a puff of white smoke far away.

'Stand firm,' said Peter, 'and wave like mad!'

'It's no good, they won't see us!' said Bobbie.

The train came faster and faster and Bobbie ran forward.

'Keep off the line!' said Peter fiercely.

'Not yet! Not yet!' cried Bobbie, and waved her flags right over the line. The front of the engine looked black and enormous. Its voice was loud and harsh.

'Oh stop, stop, stop!' cried Bobbie. The engine must have heard her, for it slackened speed swiftly and stopped dead. Bobbie still waved her flags, as Peter ran to meet the engine driver. Then she collapsed across the line.

'Gone off in a faint, poor little girl,' said the engine driver, 'and no wonder!'

They took her back to the station in the train, and she gradually came to life and began to cry.

At the station they were cheered and

praised like heroes and their ears got very red.

'Let's go home,' said Bobbie, thinking what might have happened to the people.

'It was us that saved them!' said Peter.

'We never got any cherries, did we?' said Bobbie. The others thought her rather heartless.

For Valour

There is a good deal about Roberta in this story. That is because there are all sorts of things about her that I love.

She was anxious to make other people happy. And she could keep a secret. She never said anything that would let her mother know how much she wondered what she was unhappy about. That was not as easy as you might think.

Another thing about Roberta was that she tried to help people. She wanted to help the Russian gentleman to find his wife and child. So she decided to ask the old gentleman. She got her chance one day.

The railway decided to make a presentation of three gold watches to the children, for their brave action in saving the train. There was a little ceremony at the station. The old gentleman was there, and Peter made a modest speech saying, 'What we did wasn't anything really – at least, it was awfully exciting, and thank you all very much!'

Bobbie asked the old gentleman if they could talk to him in private. So they did, and Bobbie explained about the Russian – 'Mr Sczcepansky – you call it Shepansky.' The old gentleman had heard of him, and had read his book.

'A noble book! So your mother took him in. She must be a very good woman,' he said.

Then he asked the children their names, and all sorts of questions. Just then Phyllis came in (very carefully, because her bootlace was coming undone). She was carrying a tin can and a thick slice of bread and butter which Perks had given her.

'Afternoon tea!' she announced proudly.

Ten days later, the old gentleman came to their home, through the fields.

'Good news!' he said. 'I've found your Russian's wife and child. I've come to tell him!'

Bobbie raced on ahead to be the first with the news. Mother's face lit up and she spoke a few quick French words. The Russian sprang up with a cry of love and longing and gratefully kissed Mother's hand. Then he sank into his chair, covered his face with his hands, and sobbed.

Bobbie crept away. She did not want to see the others just then. When she came back, the old gentleman gave all three children a big box of chocolates each.

The old gentleman seemed to be able to talk French and English at almost the same time, and so did Mother. The Russian's few belongings were packed and they saw him off at the station.

As they came back, Mother seemed very tired. Phyllis was talking about the Russian's baby, and how it must have grown since he saw it last.

'I wonder if Father will think I've grown!' said Phyllis, bouncing.

Bobbie said, 'Come on, Phil, I'll race you to the gate!'

You know why Bobbie did that. Mother only thought Bobbie was tired of walking slowly. Even mothers, who love you better than anyone else, don't always understand everything.

The Terrible Secret

One day, when Mother was writing, Bobbie brought her some tea. Mother said, 'Bobbie, you children aren't forgetting Father, are you? You never talk about him now.'

'Yes, we do, Mother, when we're by ourselves. Only we thought it made you unhappy to speak about him.'

'No, Bobbie dear,' said Mother, putting her arm around her. 'I'll tell you. Father and I have had a great sorrow – worse than you could ever think of – but it would be much worse if you were to forget him!'

'I promised not to ask questions,' Bobbie said in a very little voice, 'but will the trouble last always?'

'No!' said Mother. 'The worst will be over when Father comes home to us. Now I must get back to my work.' She gave Bobbie a last squeeze. 'Don't say anything to the others.'

The next day the children were gardening, when Peter fell over a rake and hurt his foot. It was an accident, but Bobbie felt it was partly her fault. So, when Peter had to stay indoors, she went down to ask Perks for any magazines people had left on the train. Perks wrapped them up in an old newspaper for her to carry.

She had to wait at the level crossing for a train to pass, so she rested the parcel on the top of the gate and looked at the printing on the paper.

Suddenly she clutched the parcel — it seemed like a horrible dream. She read on, but the bottom of the column was torn off. She never remembered how she got home. She went to her room and locked the door. Then she undid the parcel, and read the column again. Her face was burning, but her hands felt icy cold.

'So now I know!' she said.

What she had read was headed, '*End of the Trial. Sentence.*' The man who had been tried was her father. The verdict was 'Guilty'. The sentence was 'Five years, Penal Servitude.'

'Oh Daddy!' she whispered. 'It's not true! I don't believe it! You never did it! Never, never, never!'

There was a hammering on the door. 'It's me,' said Phyllis. 'Tea's ready. Come along down!'

Bobbie struggled through tea, pretending she had a headache. Then she went upstairs to her mother.

She did not know what to say. At first she just cried her mother's name bitterly, over and over again. Her mother held her close and waited. Then she pulled out the piece of newspaper and pointed to her father's name.

'Oh Bobbie!' Mother cried. 'You don't believe Daddy did it, do you?'

'*No*!' Bobbie almost shouted.

'That's right. It's *not* true. They've shut him up in prison, but he's done nothing wrong.'

'Why didn't you tell me?'

'Are you going to tell the others?'

'No!'

'Why?'

'Because...' Bobbie started, then faltered to a stop.

'Exactly,' said Mother. 'So you can understand why I didn't tell you. We two must help each other to be brave.'

And then her mother told Bobbie how the men who had come to see Father that night had arrested him for selling State secrets to the Russians. There were some letters found in Father's desk that made it look true. But Father had a man under him in the office who was jealous and wanted his job. Father thought he must have put them there, but he could not prove it.

'Couldn't we explain all that to somebody?'

'Nobody will listen, I've tried,' said Mother. 'All we can do is to be brave and patient, and pray, Bobbie dear.'

A week later Bobbie wrote a letter to her old gentleman, telling him everything, and sending the newspaper cutting.

'Think if it was *your* Daddy, how you would feel. Oh do, *do* help me. With love, I remain, your affectionate little friend Roberta.'

The Hound in the Red Jersey

The next day the grammar school boys were going on a paper chase, and the children wanted to watch. They decided to go up to the top of the cutting by the tunnel, to get a good view.

Workmen were still clearing away the landslip from the line when the 'hare' came

by. He was a big boy with dark hair, carrying a shoulder bag of torn paper to lay a trail. He ran off into the mouth of the tunnel.

Then came the 'hounds', following the trail of torn paper, down the wooden steps, into the tunnel. The last one wore a red jersey.

The children scrambled across the top to see them come out at the other end. It seemed a long time before the hare came panting out of the tunnel, and, after him, the hounds, in twos and threes, all very slow and tired.

'There's still one more to come,' said Peter, counting. 'The one in the red jersey.'

They waited, but he did not come.

'Suppose he's had an accident! He might be lying there helpless in the path of an engine!' said Peter dramatically.

'Don't talk like a book!' said Bobbie.

They set off into the tunnel. You had to walk on stepping stones and gravel, on a path that curved downwards from the shining metals to the wall. Slimy trickles of water ran down the sickly green bricks. Their voices sounded hollow and the tunnel gradually got darker. Peter lit a candle he happened to have in his pocket.

Then they heard a humming sound along the wires by the track.

'It's a train!'

'Which line?'

'Let me go back!' said Phyllis, frightened.

'Don't be a coward! You're quite safe!' said Bobbie. Peter pushed them into a damp, dark recess in the wall.

The train roared towards them, its dragon eyes of fire growing brighter every instant.

And now, with a rush and a roar, and a rattle, and a long dazzling flash of lighted carriage windows, a smell of smoke and a blast of hot air, the train hurtled by, clanging and jangling and echoing in the arched roof.

'Oh!' said the children, all together, in a whisper.

'Suppose the boy with the red jersey was in the way of the train!' said Phyllis.

'We've got to go and see,' said Peter.

About a hundred and fifty yards on they saw a gleam of red. There, by the line, was the red jerseyed hound, his back against the wall, his arms limp and his eyes shut.

'Is that red blood? Is he killed?' squeaked Phyllis.

'No, he's only fainted,' said Peter.

'What on earth can we do?'

Peter rubbed the boy's hands. Phyllis splashed milk from their picnic bottle on his forehead.

Bobbie said, 'Oh look up, speak to me. For my sake, speak!' (Which was what people always said in books when somebody fainted.)

What Bobbie brought Home

At last the boy sighed, opened his eyes and said in a very small voice, 'Chuck it!'

'Drink this!'

'What is it?'

'It's only milk. Fear not, you are in the hands of friends!' said Peter.

'I believe I've broken my leg,' said the boy with a groan. 'I tripped on these wires. How did you get here?'

'We saw you hadn't come out of the tunnel, so we came in to look for you. We're a rescue party!' said Peter proudly.

'You've got some pluck!' the boy said, and shut his eyes again.

Peter and Phyllis set off for the signal box near the tunnel to fetch help. Bobbie chose to stay with the 'hound' in the dark. It seemed a long time, and they held hands for comfort. Bobbie managed somehow to cut the laces on his boot and ease the swollen leg. Then men from a nearby farm came, with a hurdle, and carried the 'hound' to Three Chimneys.

Their mother thought they had brought a *dog* home — till she saw the hound was only a boy.

'Couldn't we keep him till he's better, Mother?' begged Peter. 'It'd be ripping to have another chap to talk to!'

'We'll see,' said Mother. It turned out that Jim (that was the hound's name) had no mother of his own, and lived with his grandfather. His school was closing for the holidays. So Mother thought it could be arranged.

You will never guess who Jim's grandfather turned out to be.

Yes, it was the old gentleman!

When he found out what Mother had done, he knew that she could not afford it, so he made Mother 'Matron of Three Chimneys Hospital', with a proper salary. He sent lots of food and two of his own servants, to help with the work.

Jim and Peter became great friends. But Jim never forgot how kind Roberta had been to him in the tunnel, and that she had been as brave as any boy.

When Jim's grandfather came, he spoke to Roberta about her letter.

'When I read your father's case in the paper, I had my doubts,' he said. 'Since I've known who you were, I've been trying to find out things. And I have hopes! Keep our secret a little longer! Don't upset your mother with false hopes.'

Whether it was a false hope or not, it lighted up Bobbie's little face like a candle in a Japanese lantern.

Jim taught Peter to play chess and dominoes and his leg got better and better. Life at Three Chimneys was nice and quiet, but also rather dull. They hardly seemed Railway Children any more, because they spent most of the time at home. But they still waved at the 9.15 and sent their love to Father by it.

'I wish something wonderful would happen,' said Bobbie dreamily.

And something wonderful did happen, four days afterwards. (According to fairy tales, it ought to be three days after, but this is not a fairy tale.)

Having servants in the house to do everything made it seem a long time since that morning when they had burned the bottom out of the kettle. It was September now, and the turf on the slope was dry and crisp.

'Hurry up!' said Peter. 'Or we shall miss the 9.15.' Phyllis stumbled over her bootlace as they all ran, slithering on the grass and waving their handkerchiefs, shouting, 'Take our love to Father!'

The old gentleman waved from his carriage window. He always waved. But today *everybody* waved – handkerchiefs, papers and hands from every window! The train swept by and left the children looking at each other.

'Well!' said Peter.

'Well!' said Roberta.

'WELL!' said Phyllis.

To the children it seemed as though the train was alive.

'I thought the old gentleman was trying to explain something to us with his newspaper,' said Bobbie.

'Explain what?' asked Peter.

'I don't know, but I feel awfully funny, as if something was going to happen.'

Later on in the morning, Bobbie still felt funny. She decided to go for a walk down to the station.

On her way, several of the villagers greeted her. The old lady from the Post Office gave her a kiss and a hug and said, 'God bless you, dear!'

The blacksmith said, 'Good morning, Missie! I wish you joy, that I do.'

The Station Master wrung her hand warmly and said, 'The 11.54's a bit late.'

Even the Station Cat gave Bobbie a special purr and rubbed round her stockings.

Bobbie wondered why everyone was so kind today. Finally Perks came out, holding a newspaper, and said, 'One I must have, Miss, on a day like this!' and kissed her cheek.

'A day like *what*?' asked Bobbie, but before he could answer, the 11.54 steamed into the station.

Of course, *you* know what was going to happen, but Bobbie was not so clever. She felt eager, confused and expectant, without knowing what she expected.

Only three people got out of the 11.54. A farmer's wife with a basket box of live chicks. A lady with several brown paper parcels. And a third – ?

'Oh, my Daddy, my Daddy!' That scream went like a knife into the hearts of everybody on the train, and people put their heads out to see a tall, thin, pale man, and a little girl clinging to him with arms and legs, while his arms went tightly around her.

As they went up the road, her father said, 'You must go in by yourself, Bobbie, and tell Mother, quite quietly, it's all right. They've caught the man who did it. Everyone knows now it wasn't your Daddy.'

'I always knew it wasn't!' said Bobbie. 'Me and Mother and our old gentleman!'

So Bobbie went into the house to tell Mother that the sorrow, the struggle, and the parting were over, and Father had come home.

Father walked in the garden, looking at the flowers, the first he had seen for a long time, and waited.

Then the door opened. Bobbie called, 'Come in, Daddy! Come in!'

The door shut. I think we will not follow them. I think it will be best for us to go quickly and quietly away. And from the end of the field, among the grass and wild flowers, take one last look at the white house, where neither we, nor anybody else, are wanted now.

Stories . . .
that have stood the test of time

SERIES 740
LADYBIRD CHILDREN'S CLASSICS

Treasure Island

Swiss Family Robinson

Secret Garden

A Journey to the
Centre of the Earth

The Three Musketeers

Gulliver's Travels

The Lost World

King Solomon's Mines

Around the World
in Eighty Days

A Christmas Carol

The Wind in the Willows

The Last of the Mohicans

The Happy Prince
and other stories

Peter Pan

Oliver Twist

The Railway Children

Kidnapped

A Little Princess

Black Beauty

Alice in Wonderland

Tom Sawyer

Little Women

SERIES 741 – LEGENDS

Aladdin & his wonderful lamp

Ali Baba & the forty thieves

Famous Legends (Book 2)

Robin Hood

King Arthur and the
Knights of the Round Table

SERIES 742 – FABLES

Aesop's Fables (Book 1)

Aesop's Fables (Book 2)

La Fontaine's Fables:
The Fox turned Wolf

SERIES SL – LARGE FORMAT

Gulliver's Travels

Aesop's Fables

SERIES 872
MYSTERY & ADVENTURE

Ghostly Tales

SERIES 841
HORROR CLASSICS

Dracula

Frankenstein

The Mummy

The strange case of
Dr Jekyll & Mr Hyde

Hound of the Baskervilles

Ladybird titles cover a wide range of subjects and reading ages.
Write for a free illustrated list from the publishers :
LADYBIRD BOOKS LTD Loughborough Leicestershire England
and USA – LADYBIRD BOOKS INC Lewiston Maine 04240